Carrie Anne in

TURTLE BOAT BATTLE

By David Lee

Copyright

Bezzle Books
1492 Lake Murray Boulevard
Columbia, South Carolina 29212

This is a work of fiction. Names, characters, places, and incidents are a product of the author's imagination. Locales and public names are sometimes used for atmospheric purposes. Any resemblance to actual people, living or dead, or to businesses, companies, events, institutions, or locales is completely coincidental.

Illustrations by teritoristudio.com.

Carrie Anne in Korea: Turtle Boat Battle / David Lee. — 1st print ed.

ISBN 978-0-9894565-8-6

Table of Contents

Chapter 1

Flames licked at the sides of the boat. Carrie Anne stood outlined by the fire, her features sketched against the dark interior of the ship.

"Jump!" Lauren, her best friend, called from the water. "Carrie Anne, you have to jump!"

In the corner of her eye, Carrie Anne could see the captain slumped over the tiller of the boat, ready to sail it into the teeth of the advancing fleet.

"Go!" shouted the captain. His men had already abandoned the doomed vessel and were swimming in the salty water of Noryang Strait, the thin strip of ocean that separated Namhae Island from the Korean peninsula.

"I think we have to." Cristoph, the son of the German ambassador, offered his hand to Carrie Anne. "There's nothing we can do."

Carrie Anne looked over the water. Boats filled the small channel separating Namhae Island from the coast of Korea. According to the captain, more than five hundred Japanese warships were advancing toward them.

Their ship had been hit by cannons. Some of the cannon balls had been heated so that they instantly set fire to any wood they touched. Even their heavily armored boat could not withstand the combined force of the Japanese fleet alone.

Carrie Anne's hand went to her wounded arm. Blood seeped through the heavy, blue fabric of her pea coat. She had been injured during the bombardment.

Their ship wouldn't be alone for long, said the captain. Already, the combined forces of Korean Admiral Yi and his Chinese allies had set sail to intercept the Japanese fleet.

Carrie Anne could see the sails of the Korean fleet on the opposite horizon.

But Admiral Yi's ships would not arrive in time to save their wrecked vessel.

The ocean rocked their ship. Carrie Anne nearly fell into the water. A loose cannon ball rolled by her foot, dropping into the sea with a splash that was barely audible over the crackling of the fire raging throughout the ship.

The captain shouted at them to jump. He remained at his station at the tiller, steering the ship. Carrie Anne wondered when she would ever meet a braver man.

"Carrie Anne?" said Cristoph.

"I don't think I can swim," said Carrie Anne, holding her arm.

"Then you'll have to trust me," said Cristoph. He grinned at her, trying to make light of their desperate situation.

But could she trust him? Carrie Anne wondered. Did she really have a choice?

Taking Cristoph's hand, Carrie Anne jumped into the ocean.

The cold water sent chills through her body. It was the middle of winter. Carrie Anne worried that they would freeze before they could swim to safety.

She broke through the surface of the water, sputtering. In the distance, she could see Lauren and the other sailors swimming toward the oncoming Korean vessels.

She couldn't find Cristoph.

Panic set in as she kicked, treading water in the frozen ocean.

Finally she saw Cristoph swimming, not toward her but away, toward the shore.

Carrie Anne realized with a sickening feeling that Cristoph had abandoned her. Her suspicions about him had been right. He couldn't be trusted. She would have to sink or swim on her own.

Carrie Anne turned as she heard the wrenching of wood against wood.

The brave captain had sailed the turtle ship into the oncoming Japanese vessels. The proud dragon on the head of the ship seemed to breathe flames as fire escaped the burning vessel.

A Japanese warship had tried to turn, too late. The Korean turtle boat hit the enemy ship, opening a gaping hole in its side. Water hissed and boiled as the burning turtle boat began to sink, taking the Japanese warship with it to the bottom of the narrow strait.

The history books had it all wrong, thought Carrie Anne. The basic information might be correct, but how could the books ever convey what a battle was truly like or what it felt like to face your own death?

Carrie Anne, a diplomat's daughter blessed with the ability to travel in time, had used her gift of time-sight to look into the history of Namhae Island. Now, trapped between the Korean and Japanese fleets, floating in the freezing waters of Noryang Strait, Carrie Anne wished she had not. She wished she had never agreed to join the treacherous Cristoph on this journey. If she had stayed home, she wouldn't be in the salty sea water, swimming with an injured arm, about to drown.

Chapter 2

SEVEN HOURS EARLIER

Carrie Anne's adventures on Namhae Island began like any other normal day.

Well, almost normal.

At 5:20 in the morning, Carrie Anne's phone started buzzing. It nearly fell off the nightstand. She slapped it as though it was an alarm clock.

Someone was texting her. Whoever it was had woken Carrie Anne from a vivid dream. She was being chased through the streets of Insadong, the art district of Seoul, by a palace guard.

7

Carrie Anne longed to go back to sleep, to see how the dream would end, but her phone kept buzzing insistently.

Only one person would be texting her so early in the morning: her best friend Lauren Saint Laurent who, for whatever reason, was an incredibly early riser.

Carrie Anne pushed a button on the side of the phone, bringing the lighted screen to her blurry eyes.

Carrie Anne swiped a thumb across the phone, bringing up the message. Even though they weren't talking directly, Carrie Anne still read the text in Lauren's French accent.

"Get up lazy!" wrote Lauren. "We're going 2 German Village."

"Where?" Carrie Anne texted back. Didn't Lauren know they were in Korea? How exactly did Lauren propose that they go to a German village?

It hadn't been that long since her friend had arrived in Korea. Lauren's father was the French Ambassador. Did she already know something that Carrie Anne didn't?

Carrie Anne's phone buzzed in her hand as Lauren replied. "On Namhae Island. German Village." A link followed the short message.

Carrie Anne pushed the link and waited as her phone pulled up a tourist website.

A colorful map showed a picture of Namhae Island, locating it on the southernmost coast of Korea. Several bright dots indicated the various attractions the island offered, including, to Carrie Anne's surprise, a dot belonging to a place called German Village. Carrie Anne touched the dot, bringing up a page with pictures and text describing the village.

From the pictures, it looked as though a village in Germany had been picked up and dropped gently on a hillside in Korea. Houses lined with red-tiled roofs and neat gardens sat in little rows.

The website said the village had been built by Koreans who'd lived and worked in Germany and who had missed their adopted homeland so much that, on returning to Korea, they had recreated German life in an out-of-the-way town overlooking the ocean.

Carrie Anne wondered what they thought about their idyllic village becoming a tourist attraction.

The website also said that the village had been built at the turn of the century, so it was hardly a place to use Carrie Anne's special talent.

Carrie Anne wasn't just the daughter of an important diplomat. Carrie Anne was special. She'd been given a great gift: the ability to see back in time. During her travels in Egypt, a Coptic Christian priest blessed Carrie Anne with time-sight.

Aside from her family, only Lauren knew about Carrie Anne's special ability.

But why would Lauren want Carrie Anne to use the ability to go back in time just to see a new place like the German Village?

Carrie Anne sent Lauren a one-word message, "Why?"

Lauren didn't take long in responding, "Cristoph invited us!!!"

Carrie Anne rolled her eyes. Now it all made sense. Lauren had taken an interest in Cristoph Landers, the son of a German diplomat living in Seoul.

Cristoph and Lauren attended the same school, the Lycée Français, a famous international school in Seoul's French district. Cristoph and Lauren had become good friends. Carrie Anne suspected that Lauren wished the friendship would develop into something more. Lauren "like" liked him.

As Carrie Anne processed this information, a new message arrived from Lauren, "C's grandparents are staying in German Village. C wants to visit them."

It was obvious to Carrie Anne that Lauren wouldn't be put off. The only question remaining was why Lauren had woken her up at 5:20 in the morning to tell Carrie Anne about their plans for the day.

Carrie Anne wrote back, "OK when?"

"Now!" came the immediate reply. "We're waiting outside with a taxi."

Carrie Anne sat straight up. Could Lauren possibly be serious? What about planning? What about the train tickets?

As if in reply to her questions, a notification popped up on her phone. Carrie Anne punched up the notice, which came from her Korean Railways app. The app showed that Carrie Anne had been booked on the 6:00 train out of Seoul.

She stared at the ticket, running a mental calculation of the time it would take to get to the train station from their apartment: about ten minutes at this time of the morning, then a five minute run to the train.

That meant Carrie Anne had only fifteen minutes to get ready.

She sprinted to the closet, wondering what to wear. What does one wear to a German village located in Korea? If the weather had been warmer, she might've been tempted to pack a swimsuit. But the late spring temperatures had yet to rise, and the ocean in Korea could be chilly even on the warmest summer days.

Carrie Anne opted for a long dress over stockings. In a nod to the ocean, she grabbed her blue pea coat, fastening the double-breasted buttons nimbly.

And what to do about her hair? There was simply no time to fix it.

Carrie Anne did the next best thing. She snagged her favorite hat, a beret, off its customary peg.

Shutting the closet door, Carrie Anne grabbed her small clutch and shoved it unceremoniously into the pea coat's overlarge front pocket. As ready as she could be, Carrie Anne headed downstairs, taking the steps in twos in her stockinged feet.

Her shoes, of course, as with all Korean households except the most stubborn foreigners, were located in the small foyer leading into the house. No one in Korea wore shoes inside the house, mainly because most Koreans sat and slept and ate on the floor. Not to mention, their heating arose from copper pipes built into the floor though which hot water cycled. Any mud tracked into the house would literally bake on the warm floors.

As Carrie Anne hit the bottom of the stairs, she noticed a light coming from the kitchen.

She was not surprised. The only person who rose earlier than Lauren was Carrie Anne's father, John Alcorn Cassat, a diplomat attached to the American Embassy in Seoul.

Carrie Anne darted into the kitchen.

Her sudden appearance, however, was a surprise to her father who'd no doubt gotten used to his daughter's habit of sleeping as late as possible.

"Daddy," she said, breathless from the rush, "can I go to Namhae Island with Lauren and her friend Cristoph?"

Her father raised an eyebrow, "Cristoph? Isn't that a boy's name?"

Carrie Anne smiled. Her father could be so over-protective sometimes. But he had nothing to fear on that account. Lauren might be "heads-over" for Cristoph, but he wasn't her type.

"Cristoph is the son of Ambassador Landers, from Germany," said Carrie Anne.

"Ah," said her father, "Kristine's boy? Well, I suppose she's the type to have raised him properly."

"I'm sure she did, Daddy."

Her father drummed his fingers on his coffee mug. "When will you be home?"

Carrie Anne's eyes strayed toward the ceiling as she calculated. She blew a stray strand of auburn hair out of her face. It was a good four or five hours to the island, and Cristoph wanted to visit with his grandparents.

"Probably not till late tonight," said Carrie Anne. "Maybe we'll catch the last train back?"

John Cassat frowned. As a diplomat, he was used to tough negotiations, especially when his daughter was involved.

"You're still only twelve-years old," he said.

"A responsible twelve, you always say," Carrie Anne responded.

A hint of a smile creased the corners of her father's eyes. "Make sure I keep saying it, right?"

Carrie Anne nodded.

"Catch the second-to-last train," said her father. "Don't get stuck overnight."

"Check!" said Carrie Anne. She pecked her father a kiss on the cheek and took off out the front door before he could change his mind.

On the curb outside, just as she'd promised, Lauren sat in a taxicab waiving to Carrie Anne out of the window. Cristoph sat next to her, smiling.

"Hurry up," Lauren said in her pert, French accent. "We're going to miss our train!"

Postcards from Korea:

KTX Bullet Train

Chapter 3

I thought we were never going to make it," said Cristoph. He was breathing hard, sitting on a bench opposite from Carrie Anne and Lauren.

Lauren had thoughtfully selected family seats, so they could all sit together. Family seats were located in the middle of each carriage. Two benches had been turned to face each other with a table placed between them.

Across the aisle, a family of four occupied the other family seats. The mother and father were eating an impromptu breakfast while their children stared at electronic screens.

Carrie Anne's stomach rumbled, reminding her that she hadn't had time to eat before rushing out of the house. She would have to keep an eye out for the food cart.

The steady thump-a-thump of wheels running on tracks disappeared as the high-speed train picked up momentum, crossing over the Han River.

At top speed, the train might go 300 kilometers per hour.

Carrie Anne shook her head. In her travels around the world, she had learned to think in metric measurements. She converted the speed into her native miles per hour, which made it close to 200 miles per hour!

"I still don't understand," said Cristoph, "how we managed to catch the train."

"That," said Lauren, "is just one of Carrie Anne and my secrets."

Lauren smiled sweetly.

Cristoph turned a questioning gaze on Carrie Anne.

She swallowed hard. Lauren had said it was "one" of their secrets. Carrie Anne worried that Lauren might be hinting about her big secret: time-sight—the ability to travel in time.

Still, with Lauren turning silent and Cristoph looking to her for an explanation, Carrie Anne had to say something.

"We used the tunnels under the station to go directly to the tracks." Carrie Anne shrugged as if it was no big deal.

In fact, the man who ran Seoul Station, Mr. Lee, had personally shown them the tunnels on their way to a memorable adventure in Gyeongju. He had since given the girls permission to use the tunnels in times of need.

Cristoph raised his eyebrows, looking suitably impressed.

Lauren took up the story, telling about how she'd met Carrie Anne in front of Seoul station after so many years apart and how Carrie Anne had practically dragged her into the dark bowels of the train station (where she thought they would be murdered!) only to find themselves, at the very last second, right in front of their train.

Lauren told about their journey to Gyeongju. Thankfully, she omitted certain parts that couldn't be told without revealing Carrie Anne's secret.

Time-sight. Lauren had accidentally discovered Carrie Anne's secret ability during their trip to Gyeongju. Afterward, the two girls had used time-sight to travel back in time. They'd rescued a treasured lion statue belonging to Bulguksa Temple. As a result, Carrie Anne and Lauren had become minor celebrities in Korea.

A few weeks earlier, photographers had been camped out on Carrie Anne's doorstep, waiting to take pictures.

Thankfully, the paparazzi had grown bored and moved on. Other girls might have been happy to remain in the spotlight, but Carrie Anne didn't mind the lack of attention.

The Coptic Christian priests in Egypt who had blessed her with time-sight had asked her to keep it a secret. She had promised.

Using her time-sight was simple. By crossing her fingers, Carrie Anne could open a window to the past.

The gift had been more than she expected, though, as she and Lauren had learned.

Not only could Carrie Anne look into the past, she could step into it. She could touch, taste, and smell the past. She could speak with historic figures in their own languages.

In fact, Carrie Anne still didn't know the full extent of her abilities.

In Gyeongju, she and Lauren had been in grave danger, looking down the barrel of a loaded gun. Carrie Anne believed that if she were injured in the past, she could have died for real.

The realization shocked her.

She needed time to practice, to figure out what she was capable of doing.

It had been difficult to practice in Seoul, especially with the paparazzi hounding them for photos.

Carrie Anne hoped that this trip might be different. Outside of Seoul, she might have some privacy and a chance to get a handle on her abilities.

For instance, even though Carrie Anne could look back in time by crossing her fingers, she couldn't yet control how far back she went.

The time-sight seemed to have a mind of its own when it came to deciding what to show her from the past.

Carrie Anne knew that the Coptic priest had given her the gift of time-sight for a reason. She couldn't use the gift for selfish purposes. They'd given her the gift so that she could help people.

Carrie Anne returned to Lauren and Cristoph's conversation just as Lauren was concluding, "That's how we returned the lion statute to Dabotap Pagoda."

"Brilliant," said Cristoph.

Lauren beamed. "It was not much. Anyone would have done the same."

"Brilliant," said Cristoph again.

If he smiled any harder, Carrie Anne feared that his mouth might get stuck that way.

Lauren and Cristoph continued to regard each other in silence.

Carrie Anne cleared her throat, adding, "So, Cristoph, your grandparents live on Namhae Island?"

Cristoph blinked as though he were waking up from a dream. He recovered quickly. His training as the son of a diplomat kicked in. Turning his attention to Carrie Anne, he gave an enthusiastic description of the island.

"It's a brilliant place actually," he said. "There's a butterfly preserve on this mountain with more butterflies than you can count. There's this odd little museum dedicated to garlic that has a display featuring the bear who ate garlic and became a woman. Do you know the story?"

In fact, Carrie Anne did know the tale, having read several histories of the Korean peninsula.

Legend told of a bear who, at the instruction of the gods, had become a woman by eating garlic in a cave. She later gave birth to Tangun, the first Korean.

Although the tale seemed a little strange to an American like Carrie Anne, she'd been moved by the bear's desire to rise above her animal nature enough to undertake a really bitter task—eating all that garlic. Unsurprisingly, her companion, a tiger, had found the task too demanding and had quit. It was no wonder that the son of the bear-woman became such a strong man, able to create an entire nation. Really, the story was touching in its own way.

Carrie Anne nodded as Cristoph continued to describe Namhae Island.

"There's a replica of a warship and a famous village where the rice paddies descend in hundreds of small terraces down the side of the mountain. That village is guarded by an ancient stone."

Lauren nudged Carrie Anne's elbow. Carrie Anne took the hint. That village might be an excellent place to practice her time-sight.

"And of course," said Cristoph, "there's the German village where my grandparents live."

Carrie Anne's curiosity got the better of her, "Why do they live all the way in Namhae? Why not closer to you in Seoul?" Actually, what she really wanted to ask was why his grandparents lived in Korea at all? Why not remain in Germany?

"My grandmother is Korean," said Cristoph.

Carrie Anne couldn't conceal the look of surprise on her face.

"Didn't you know?" Cristoph smiled. "Don't I look Korean enough for you?"

Cristoph was teasing Carrie Anne.

Inwardly she cringed. She too had been raised by a diplomat. To make such a clumsy error about someone's ethnicity was practically inexcusable.

Cristoph did not let Carrie Anne off the hook. He continued, "As for why they live so far away," he said, "I suppose you're thinking it's because they can't stand my mother?"

Cristoph's eyes twinkled as though he was joking, but Carrie Anne couldn't tell if part of him might be serious.

Carrie Anne thought nothing of the sort about his mother. But her question had been badly phrased. And now Cristoph must think she was prying into his family business.

Carrie Anne's head sunk into her shoulders. She prepared herself for an awkward silence and an even more awkward trip. Carrie Anne wished she had never gotten out of bed. She wished she could cross her fingers, go back in time, and keep herself from saying something stupid.

But she couldn't control her time-sight any more than she could control what was turning into a horrible day.

Chapter 4

Cristoph fixed Carrie Anne with his brown eyes. His smile reminded her of the famous painting of the Mona Lisa that she'd seen when her father had been stationed in Paris.

The train continued to run silently down the tracks. The countryside raced by, leaving a series of bright green splotches where the new rice shoots were growing in the flooded paddies.

Lauren didn't seem to notice the conversation or how it had stalled. She rummaged through her big red purse.

Carrie Anne wished that her friend would help her out or at least change the subject.

At that moment, the door to the carriage opened and the meal cart came down the narrow aisle, pushed by an older Korean man in a railway uniform. Carrie Anne remembered her first encounter with that uniform— when she had run into Mr. Lee headfirst while racing to catch a train. She'd been lucky to meet the man who ran Seoul Station and to learn of the tunnels underneath. She felt just as lucky now to see the meal cart. Not only was she hungry, the cart would provide a useful distraction.

Carrie Anne snagged a meal box from the porter, handing him her phone.

He touched the back of her phone to a small black box near the handle of the cart. The box beeped and coughed up a small receipt of purchase. Carrie

Anne never ceased to be amazed by the technology in Korea.

A computer chip, called a money card, was attached to the back of her phone. The card connected to a bank account that Carrie Anne's father filled from time to time with her allowance. Carrie Anne could use the money card to purchase a meal, as she just had, or to pay for a taxi or for a train ticket. Even at twelve-years-old, the money card made Carrie Anne independent and able to travel easily around Seoul or around the entire Korean peninsula.

While the money card could provide material comforts, like breakfast, it could not provide the sort of moral support that Carrie Anne needed right then to deal with an awkward conversation.

After Carrie Anne had pulled apart her bamboo chopsticks, rolling them together in her hand to smooth away any splinters, Cristoph answered

Carrie Anne's invasive questions about his family.

"My grandmother worked in Germany as a nurse where she met my grandfather. They fell in love and all the rest."

Lauren finally chimed in, "Oh, how sweet!"

Carrie Anne resisted the urge to roll her eyes, thinking how very unhelpful Lauren's comment had been.

Cristoph nodded, acknowledging Lauren's assessment. "When my mother was assigned to Korea, my grandparents decided to come as well. My grandmother wanted to live in a place that reminded her of her former village in Korea. My grandfather favored something more German. They settled in German Village and are both happy. And—" Cristoph coughed. His brown eyes twinkled. "It doesn't hurt that Namhae is as far from my mother as they can get."

Carrie had always considered Cristoph's mother, Ambassador Kristine Landers, to be a little severe. But she'd thought perhaps all older German people were like that. It surprised her to hear Cristoph talk about his mother openly. In diplomatic circles, one rarely aired the family's dirty laundry.

Judging from Cristoph's merry expression, however, it looked as though he'd told an old joke.

Cristoph continued, "It shocks you that I speak so irreverently about my mother?"

It was like he was reading her mind. Carrie Anne realized that she needed to work on controlling her facial expressions, what her father called a "poker face," if she was going to be a diplomat like John Cassat.

"I find," said Cristoph, "one has to make a choice in life, whether to cry or whether to laugh. I've chosen to laugh." He waved a hand toward Carrie Anne. "What about you?"

Carrie Anne found herself in a position where she was forced to respond. She wondered what kind of person she might be, whether she was stern like her father or Cristoph's mother, or whether she was light-hearted like Cristoph.

Lauren laughed, "Carrie Anne, you look so serious." Turning to Cristoph, Lauren added, "She is an old-soul, Cristoph. Now, stop bothering her and tell me more about the island."

As Lauren turned the conversation to more pleasant topics, Carrie Anne thought about the question. If forced to choose a term to describe herself, she would choose words like loyal and discreet.

These might be serious traits, but they seemed more valuable than joking.

Carrie Anne began to wonder about Lauren's attraction to Cristoph. Was he the sort of person who could be trusted, especially if he would share such personal information about his family?

Carrie Anne hoped she would never have to trust Cristoph to keep her secret.

Postcards from Korea:

Chapter 5

Namhae Island was as beautiful as Cristoph had described it. Their bus drove across a long suspension bridge and into the heart of the small village that connected the island to the Korean peninsula. The streets of the town were lined with restaurants offering sea food. Hawkers standing on the street waived to the bus passengers, inviting them into the restaurants.

Carrie Anne checked the time on her phone. The train had taken them to the sprawling port city of Busan, crossing the length of the country in less than three hours. From Busan, they'd caught a bus to Namhae. The bus ride had added a couple more hours. It was getting near lunch time. Carrie Anne's stomach reminded her that she'd only eaten a box meal on the train that day.

Carrie Anne spoke up. "What's the plan?" She was looking at Lauren but talking to Cristoph, who knew the island better than either of the girls. Still, Carrie Anne couldn't bring herself to address him directly just yet. She was still feeling a bit embarrassed by her mistake in the train earlier.

"I'll negotiate with a taxi driver to take us to the German village," said Cristoph. "We can grab lunch there."

He walked away in the direction of the taxi stand. Numerous drivers waited near their taxis, talking together in small groups. If Cristoph had decent haggling skills, thought Carrie Anne, he was sure to get a good rate on the taxi. Of course, they could always just pay by the meter, but sometimes it saved a little money to negotiate.

Carrie Anne guessed at how much it might cost. Then she did a small tally of their bus fare.

"You know, Lauren," said Carrie Anne, "We could almost have paid for a taxi from Busan to here by the time we paid for three bus tickets."

"*Chinjja?*" said Lauren.

Carrie Anne regarded her friend askance. That was not French she was speaking.

"It's Korean," said Lauren. "It means, 'really?!'"

"Have you been taking lessons?" asked Carrie Anne.

Lauren shrugged and hoisted her big, red purse onto one shoulder. "Father insisted."

Carrie Anne had been meaning to take lessons as well. Like everything else, it was easier said than actually done. Carrie Anne had convinced herself that by watching a few hours of Korean dramas every day, she was doing some serious language study. Yet, Lauren had easily passed her by.

Lauren didn't brag about her language skills. She was eager to talk about something much closer to her heart. She reached out and squeezed Carrie Anne's hand.

"Isn't he cute?"

Lauren's French accent was cute, but Carrie Anne wasn't so sure about Cristoph, the object of Lauren's attention.

"I don't know—" Carrie Anne began.

Lauren cut her off, not really listening. She twirled a bit of her blond hair around a finger. "I mean those brown eyes, that sharp Teutonic nose."

"Teutonic?" said Carrie Anne.

"German, I mean German nose," said Lauren, smiling at her American friend's ignorance of all things continental—that is to say, European.

Carrie Anne looked back over at Cristoph. He was waving his arms quite a bit and looking as though he were struggling mightily to win a complacent cab driver over to his side. Carrie Anne guessed that the drivers had worked out a set price between themselves already, and that price might go up for foreigners. The cab drivers of Namhae wouldn't undercut a neighbor on their price, not since they had to hang out together at the taxi stand day in and day out.

While Cristoph haggled, Carrie Anne decided to see a bit of the small town.

A sign pointed in the direction of an outdoor museum reputed to contain some relics of the famous Admiral Yi, who had fought against a Japanese fleet. In the harbor sat a full-scale replica of one of Admiral Yi's famous turtle boats.

Carrie Anne walked down the street to get a better view of the turtle ship.

Lauren came with her, babbling the whole time about Cristoph this and Cristoph that.

"I think we might be a couple," said Lauren, "although he hasn't asked me. But, who knows, we might be."

Carrie Anne wanted to say how happy she was for Lauren, but first of all, at twelve years of age, a serious relationship hardly seemed worth the effort. Maybe in another two years or so. Second of all, Carrie Anne wasn't sure that she approved of Cristoph. He hadn't exactly been rude on the train, but neither had he been gracious about her social gaffe. What's more, Carrie Anne didn't feel like she could trust him.

"Oh, Carrie Anne, look at this view!"

Lauren's sudden exclamation brought Carrie Anne out of her funk. She looked up to see the bright waters of Noryang Strait at noon. The strait was mostly empty, except for some of the typical Korean fishing boats, white dinghies with a tall cockpit, prowling up and down the coast. But these were nothing compared to the replica of the turtle boat, which sat at the edge of the sea, inviting visitors to come aboard.

Instead of the usual wooden deck, the turtle boat was covered with a protective shell that was lined with metal spikes to repel boarders.

The boat bristled with small cannons sticking out of numerous portholes along its side and even one in the mouth of a great dragon whose head rode on the front of the ship.

"Carrie Anne," said Lauren, "do it!"

"Do what?" said Carrie Anne, giving her friend a hard time. She knew what Lauren meant.

"Use your time-sight," said Lauren.

"Here?" said Carrie Anne

"Why not," said Lauren, taking Carrie Anne by the hand.

"I guess I could try," said Carrie Anne.

"I've got the taxi," said Cristoph, laying a hand on Lauren's shoulder.

Carrie Anne had already begun to cross her fingers. She heard him too late—saw him place a hand on Lauren's shoulder too late.

The three of them, Lauren, Carrie Anne, and Cristoph were staring at Noryang Strait. But instead of early May, they were wracked by a wintry breeze. And instead of a mostly empty ocean, they could see a line of boats entering the strait.

In front of them, the turtle boat remained. But it was not a replica. It was the real deal. Sailors crawled over it, tossing off lines, preparing to shove off.

Several sailors were running down the hill toward the boat when Carrie Anne and the others appeared.

"Stop!" yelled a sailor. "Who goes there?"

"Enemy spies?" said another.

"I don't know," said the first. "I think we'd best take them to the captain."

"There's no time," said the other. "Let's kill the spies here and be done with it."

Lauren and Cristoph stared at Carrie Anne in panic, especially Cristoph, who had no idea what had just happened.

"Uncross your fingers Carrie Anne!" Lauren pleaded. "Take us home."

Carrie Anne agreed. She uncrossed her fingers immediately.

They didn't move in time. They remained in the past, facing a brace of Korean sailors who moved menacingly in their direction.

Overhead, they heard a whistling sound followed by a boom. A cannon shell exploded over the channel.

The soldiers advanced toward them just as the fleet entering the strait opened fire.

Postcards from Korea:

TURTLE BOAT

Chapter 6

L et's take them to the captain," said the Korean sailor. "Let the captain decide what to do with these spies."

The sailor grabbed Cristoph roughly by the elbow, dragging him toward the turtle boat that was waiting just below them in the port.

Carrie Anne could see the anchor being lifted out of the ocean. The boat was getting ready to cast off.

Cristoph began to pull against the soldier, "Who are you and where are you taking me?"

The soldier reached for a knife at his waist.

"Cristoph!" Carrie Anne called out. "Don't fight. Just go with them."

"What's happening?" said Cristoph, allowing himself to be led by the sailor.

Carrie Anne and Lauren followed after him, with the second sailor taking up the rear, ushering them along with a series of hard shoves in the back. The sailors were anxious to get on board the boat before it shoved away from the shore.

"I'll explain later," said Carrie Anne.

The sailor pushed her up the narrow gangplank that led on board the ship. "That's enough talking from you spies!"

Lauren protested, "We are not spies! Eeek!" She squeaked when the sailor grabbed the top of her head, forcing her into the small, darkened doorway of the turtle boat.

Even in the daylight, the inside of the boat was covered in shadows. The ship did not have much light. Torches were carefully spaced throughout the cabin, since they had to be careful to keep fire away from the gunpowder that supplied their small cannons.

"Captain!" said the sailor, "We caught these spies on shore."

"Cast off!" called the captain. "Charge the cannons."

The captain was easy to spot. He was the one barking out orders. Also, among the sailors, he was the only one wearing lacquered armor. The rest were clad in loose, gray garments and went barefoot.

The captain's expensive-looking armor could only belong to someone from the noble class. The captain must be a high-ranking officer in the Korean military. Yet he looked too young and too handsome to be so important.

Carrie Anne took the initiative.

"We are not spies. We are foreign nationals and protected by law." Carrie Anne wasn't sure exactly what law protected them in that day and age. She gambled that the nobility of the captain might prevent him from harming foreigners.

The captain regarded Carrie Anne with narrowed, cat-like eyes. His young face already showed worry lines at the corners of his eyes. He brushed at his thin mustache and beard as though considering how to respond.

Through the wooden ceiling of the turtle boat, Carrie Anne could hear the thump of exploding cannon shells. The fleet entering the strait was trying to blow the turtle boat out of the water.

A great crash caused Carrie Anne to flinch. Lauren and Cristoph involuntarily ducked.

The captain stood on the rolling deck of the turtle boat as it moved into deep water, undisturbed by the battle raging around him.

Finally, he spoke. "The roof of the ceiling is armored. The shells cannot break through."

"Captain, we are not here to spy," said Carrie Anne, having recovered from the shock.

"I believe you," he said. "You do not look like spies. But you must understand, we are at war. The Japanese fleet led by General Shimazu has just entered Noryang Strait. If they break through and join forces with General Konishi, all will be lost."

Lauren spoke up, "What can you do with only one ship?"

The captain smiled. "You might be surprised." He paused to call out orders to his crew. "Besides, we will not be alone for long. Admiral Yi has learned of the Japanese attack and is massing behind us with the combined forces of Korea and our Chinese allies. If we hadn't had to land to make repairs to our boat, we would be with Admiral Yi's fleet even now."

As he spoke, a cannon ball ripped through the side of the turtle boat, missing the armored shell of the ship.

The cannon shell tore through one of the wooden columns that supported the roof. It lodged in the far side of the boat.

The wood around it burst into flames.

"Hot shot!" shouted a sailor. "They're using hot shot."

Carrie Anne could see that the cannon ball was glowing red like a coal in a fire. The enemy must have heated the ball before firing it.

The captain shouted to the crew. Buckets of water were tossed on the cannon shell and the burning side of the boat. The buckets had been held at the ready against just such an attack.

"Fire cannons!" shouted the captain.

The roar of the guns as they fired on the oncoming Japanese fleet nearly deafened Carrie Anne, though she wondered what good such small cannons could do against the large fleet.

There was no way to tell without looking through one of the small, round portholes.

Lauren shouted, "Carrie Anne!"

"What?" she said. Her head suddenly felt fuzzy.

"Your arm!"

Carrie Anne looked down. Splinters of wood stuck out of her upper arm. Blood seeped through the blue pea coat, turning its fabric a deep purple.

The shell that struck the column must have sent the wood flying into her arm.

Carrie Anne felt faint.

Chapter 7

"Sit down!" The captain ordered Carrie Anne before returning his attention to the battle.

She obeyed. Lauren and Cristoph gathered around her.

Another large clang shook the boat, where a cannon shell careened off the armored roof of the turtle ship.

"What is happening?" hissed Cristoph. His eyes were wide and demanding. His joking mood had evaporated.

Lauren explained while she examined Carrie Anne's injury. "Carrie Anne can travel in time. We only wanted to see what the past looked like. Yet here we are!"

"But how did we get here?" said Cristoph.

"We were traveling in time. When you touched my shoulder, you came with us."

Cristoph shook his head, "That's not possible."

"*Mon chèr*," said Lauren, "Let's speak less about what is possible and more about what is actually happening. Carrie Anne needs help, and we all must survive this battle. Grab that rag, will you?"

Lauren pointed at a cloth lying on the deck of the ship. It was soaked with water and looked as though it had been used to clean the barrel of a cannon. But Carrie Anne knew a little gunpowder wouldn't hurt her.

Lauren's calm during the battle impressed Carrie Anne deeply. She had made a good choice for a friend in Lauren Saint Laurent. However, Carrie

Anne was not so sure that Lauren had made a good choice in Cristoph. Could they really trust him with the secret of time-sight?

Cristoph took the cloth and handed it to Lauren who had pulled several long, bloody splinters out of Carrie Anne's arm.

Cristoph asked the obvious question, "Why can't we travel back to the future?"

Carrie Anne shook her head, "I don't know. I tried. I'm still learning how my gift works."

Cristoph laughed.

Carrie Anne couldn't believe it. Here they were, in a life and death situation, and Cristoph was laughing.

He shrugged his shoulders as if to say he couldn't help it. "It's absurd."

Lauren looked up at him with serious blue eyes, "Cristoph, help me with her coat."

Her unspoken admonition seemed to bring Cristoph to his senses.

Perhaps he realized how badly he was behaving.

"Of course," he said, growing serious again.

Slipping off the heavy pea coat, Carrie Anne gritted her teeth while Lauren bound her wound with the dirty rag.

Over Lauren's shoulder, Carrie Anne watched as the crew of the turtle boat battled valiantly, standing alone against the oncoming Japanese fleet.

Another shell burst through the wall of the boat causing the wooden timbers to catch fire.

"Hot shot!" yelled a soldier.

Before they could douse the cannon ball with water, another two shells pierced the shell of the turtle ship. Fire raged throughout the vessel.

The captain's voice rang out, "Abandon ship!"

The sailors bounded to obey. They dove out of the small door in the side of the vessel or out the window in the back near the large tiller that guided the ship. The captain hunched over the steering mechanism, pointing the ship directly toward the Japanese fleet. Flames flickered uncomfortably close to the gunpowder the crew had been using to fire their cannons.

"We should go," said Lauren. "Can you swim?"

"I don't know," said Carrie Anne.

Cristoph offered, "I will help her."

"No," said Carrie Anne. "I can make it."

Lauren shook her head. "Don't be silly, Carrie Anne. Cristoph was on the German youth swim team before coming to Korea. He could have been in the Olympics."

Cristoph's crimson red blush showed clearly on his face, which was quite a feat given how red the air had already become from the fire.

He and Lauren helped Carrie Anne to her feet.

They stumbled to the door of the boat, unused as they were to the roll of the ocean underfoot.

Carrie Anne gave one last look at the valiant young captain.

Cristoph took her hand.

"Trust me," he said, giving her a little grin.

She had no choice.

Carrie Anne jumped into the icy waters of Noryang Strait.

* * *

Now, floating in the frozen sea, Carrie Anne despaired. Lauren and the sailors were swimming toward the oncoming Korean fleet. The captain had crashed the turtle boat into the side of Japanese warship. Flames engulfed the enemy vessel. Both ships began to sink into the water.

Carrie Anne was barely managing to keep her head above water. Her wounded arm hung useless at her side. Every time she tried to use it, the pain was nearly unbearable.

And Cristoph, whom she'd been
told to trust, had abandoned her.
She'd last seen him swimming toward
the shore. Salt water sloshed into
her mouth and up her nose, burning
her sinuses. Carrie Anne watched as
the Japanese fleet approached. She
wondered whether she would freeze
to death or drown before their massive
ships ran her over.

Postcards from Korea:

NORYANG STRAIT

Chapter 8

G rab this!" a voice close to her
called out.

Carrie Anne turned her attention
away from the Japanese fleet and
the fiery wreck that marked where
the turtle boat had collided with the
warship.

A heavy board brushed her hand.

She grabbed it, kicking with her
legs to bring her chest onto the
floating wooden structure.

Next to her swam Cristoph, holding
the drifting wood steady in the water.

"I think it's a piece of the turtle
boat," said Cristoph. "I saw it right

before we jumped. I had to swim to get it."

"I thought you—" Carrie Anne stopped herself. Her teeth chattered.

"Abandoned you?" Cristoph completed her sentence. His lips, which were tinted blue from the cold water, creased into a smile. "And leave my ticket home?"

Did he take anything seriously, Carrie Anne wondered? But before she could ask or say anything else, the board lurched forward. She struggled to keep hold of it.

Cristoph was propelling the floating platform toward the oncoming Korean fleet with a series of strong kicks.

Carrie Anne added her own meager effort. She tried to kick in unison with Cristoph but could barely keep up with his quick strokes.

Together, they caught up to Lauren and matched her pace.

A small boat launched from the Korean fleet came to pick up the shipwrecked sailors. Carrie Anne, Lauren, and Cristoph were taken on board as well.

They shivered, clinging together for warmth in the bottom of the boat as heavy blankets were thrown over them.

A large Korean sailor sat at the back of the boat. He ran a hand over the top of his balding head. Though he wore the simple clothing of a sailor, Carrie Anne noticed how the rest of the crew reacted to him. The large man had the look of authority. He spoke to the wet sailors. "Did you get a good look at the Japanese fleet?"

The sailors nodded.

"Good. You will report to Admiral Yi."

Turning the small boat expertly, the bald sailor pointed the boat toward the largest ship in the Korean fleet. Carrie Anne assumed it was the flagship of Admiral Yi.

She couldn't believe her own eyes. They were about to meet one of the most famous people in all of Korean history. Carrie Anne wondered if Cristoph and Lauren appreciated the significance of the meeting that was about to take place.

Of course, it also occurred to Carrie Anne that, should they be mistaken as spies by Admiral Yi, she might find herself again thrown into the frozen water of Noryang Strait.

"Carrie Anne," Lauren whispered, "what are we to do?"

"I don't know," said Carrie Anne. "I don't know."

* * *

Admiral Yi's floating headquarters was not located on one of his famous turtle ships. Those ships, small and maneuverable, were meant for fighting up-close. Admiral Yi could not afford to rush into the fight as he might have done as a young man. As an Admiral, he had to stay back and direct the battle. This he did by use of flags. The flags had various designs that, when waved singly or in combination, sent messages to the ships in his fleet.

Just now, as Carrie Anne understood it, Admiral Yi's flags indicated that his fleet should sit back and shower the Japanese fleet with a barrage of cannon shells.

Carrie Anne stood on the deck of the flagship wearing her damaged pea coat over top of a sailor's uniform that had been loaned to her to replace her wet clothes.

She watched as a cannon from Admiral Yi's boat hit its mark, sending a Japanese ship to the bottom of Noryang Strait.

Yet the Japanese shells fell short of the Korean vessels.

"What are your orders, Admiral?" the captain of the flagship put the question to the Admiral, deferring to the great man's wishes.

Admiral Yi Sun-sin, dressed in his polished battle armor, cut an impressive figure on the deck of the ship. He was a bit shorter than Carrie Anne had imagined him, yet the authority emanating from his presence made him seem like a towering figure. Everyone in the boat looked to him, anticipating his command. Even Carrie Anne held her breath.

"Hold this position," said Admiral Yi. "The Japanese cannons cannot reach us. Yet we can attack them at will." Admiral Yi pointed a hand toward the battle. "You see that most of their ships are troop transports. They want to get in close and fight—to board our ships."

The captain stood at Admiral Yi's elbow. "I see," he said. "Admiral your order to await their fleet in the strait was a brilliant strategy."

Admiral Yi waved away the man's compliment. "If you want to admire someone, admire the simple fishermen who delivered warning that the fleet was approaching."

The captain bowed, acknowledging the Admiral's wisdom and humility.

The Admiral came to stand next to Carrie Anne. He spoke between the near-deafening roars of cannon fire. "I understand you were on the ship that intercepted the enemy fleet?"

Carrie Anne nodded in response. Though normally not a shy person, she found herself at a loss for words in the Admiral's presence.

"My cousin's son, Yi Wan, commanded the ship," he said.

Carrie Anne spoke up, "Though his turtle ship was badly damaged, he rammed one of their warships"

"Of course he did," said the Admiral. "Yi Wan's actions slowed them down, buying us precious time to prepare our trap."

Carrie Anne said nothing as she thought of her final sight of the brave captain calmly holding the weight of the tiller.

Admiral Yi continued, "I honor you for fighting at his side and welcome you aboard my ship."

A few steps away, Lauren and Cristoph stood looking out over the ocean. Lauren leaned up against the steady German.

Carrie Anne's respect for Cristoph had improved. He had saved her from the frozen water, where she would have drowned; and, though he had freaked out a little at first, he'd come to accept their situation, though not in the stoic or serious way one might expect.

As Carrie Anne looked at Cristoph, he winked at her.

She blinked in surprise. There it was again, the impish sense of humor that she'd originally found so off-putting. What had he said on the train? When faced with difficulty, you could choose to laugh or to cry. Maybe humor and joking was his way of coping with whatever life threw at him.

Maybe, just maybe, he wasn't such a bad guy after all.

"Admiral!" the captain of the flagship shouted, pointing off toward the horizon.

"What is it?" said the Admiral, moving away from Carrie Anne to see what the captain was pointing at.

The Admiral stood very still for a moment. His breath, chilled by the cold, winter air, came out in visible puffs.

Carrie Anne imagined she heard him sigh.

"Chen, you fool!" said the Admiral. Then, turning to the captain, he said, "Sound the war drums. Order the fleet to close with the Japanese. We must help Chen. Prepare for hand to hand combat."

The crew of the flagship jumped at the Admiral's command. The war drums sounded. Signal flags waived, putting the fleet in motion. Cannons rolled back. Oars dipped into the water, pulling the ship toward the Japanese.

Lauren turned to Cristoph, saying, "But I thought we wanted to stay well away from them?"

Admiral Yi's sharp ears must have overheard her comment, for he gave a brusque answer, "A Japanese vessel taunted our ally from China, challenging him to fight. He accepted the challenge. Oh, Chen, we had them trapped! Now we must go with him or Chen will be cut off."

A cannon shell from a Japanese ship whipped through the air, landing just beyond the flagship. They were out of the range of the Japanese guns no longer.

"You three had better go into my cabin," said Admiral Yi. "There will be fighting."

"We want to help, Admiral," said Carrie Anne.

The old man smiled. "A noble sentiment," he said. "Were it not for your injured arm, I might accept your service."

Carrie Anne realized that the Admiral was right. With her injury, she would only get in the way.

"I'll fight with you, sir," said Cristoph.

Lauren looked at him with a mixture of pride and horror.

"Very well," said Admiral Yi, looking Cristoph up and down approvingly. "Your first assignment is to see these two to safety."

"Aye, aye sir," Cristoph said and saluted.

Admiral Yi seemed amused by the gesture. Carrie Anne wondered whether salutes were used by the Korean navy or whether that was a later invention, perhaps of the British navy.

Admiral Yi waved Cristoph away saying, "See to it, son, and come right back. A fight is coming."

Postcards from Korea:

Chapter 9

Carrie Anne and Lauren huddled in Admiral Yi's cabin as the fighting raged outside. The shouts of Korean sailors were mixed with those of the Japanese as the boats sailed so close together, close enough to exchange cannon shots, and gun shots, and abusive language.

Cristoph burst into the room.

In his hand was a short sword. His face was scraped and bleeding. Yet he was still smiling.

"Cristoph," Lauren flung herself at him, putting her arms around his neck. "What's happening?"

Cristoph set her down, extracting himself from the neck-breaking hug.

"The battle is intense," he said, wiping his face and noticing, perhaps for the first time, the blood flowing from his cheek.

"We've had to repel boarders several times," he continued. "Some Japanese sailors managed to get on board during the last attack. They were trying to throw burning wood onto our ship, can you imagine? I think we got them all, but I had to check on you, just in case."

"We're fine," said Carrie Anne, "but how about the battle? Who's winning?"

Cristoph's grin turned into a slight frown. He scratched at his head absentmindedly with the handle of the sword. "It's difficult to say, really. It's a mass of confusion. The captain got injured, but he's back on his feet. Anyway," he grabbed the door handle, "I'd better go back."

"Be careful!" said Lauren.

The door burst open.

"Make way," someone shouted.

Admiral Yi entered the cabin followed by the captain, whose head was caked with blood from a wound just above his scalp. With them was the bald sailor who had rescued Carrie Anne out of the strait earlier. They were joined by someone Carrie Anne immediately recognized. It was Yi Wan, the captain of the turtle boat. She thought he was dead.

The door closed behind them.

Carrie Anne and Lauren crowded against the wall of the small cabin as Admiral Yi collapsed onto a bench.

Carrie Anne wondered why he would leave the fighting unsupervised. Then she saw blood pouring down the front of his armor. His right hand clutched a wound under his left arm. His jaw was firmly set in a face that had paled from loss of blood.

"Admiral," said the captain, "We must send the signal and turn command of the fleet over to one of your lieutenants."

"No," said the Admiral firmly.

"But father," said the bald sailor, "we have won. Victory is yours."

"Send no signal, son. Change no flags," said the Admiral. "Our men might lose heart. We must fight on. We must stop the Japanese invasion decisively, here and now. My orders remain the same. Pursue the Japanese fleet and destroy it."

"But, sir—" the Admiral's son protested.

Admiral Yi cut him off. "We are about to win the war—keep beating the war drums. Do not announce my death."

Admiral Yi's eyes closed. He slumped onto the bench. The life had gone out of him.

The son nodded grimly, running a hand over his bald head. He spoke quietly, "I will obey you in life and in death, father."

He strode out of the cabin.

Carrie Anne, through tears that she wasn't even aware had formed in her eyes, looked at Yi Wan, who was just as stricken with grief as she was.

Only Cristoph seemed unaffected by the scene. He said, "It doesn't matter what the Admiral says, if the men don't see him on deck, they'll know something's wrong."

"Cristoph!" Lauren sounded appalled that he would speak about the dead that way.

"He's right," said Yi Wan. "We have to convince both our men and the Japanese that Admiral Yi yet lives."

Lauren said, "But what can we do?"

"His armor," said Carrie Anne. "Everyone knows what Admiral Yi's armor looks like. Someone could wear it."

Yi Wan nodded, acknowledging Carrie Anne's plan. "It is a time of war. We will do what must be done."

Turning to Cristoph, Yi Wan said, "Help me."

Carefully and respectfully, they removed the polished, lacquered armor and helmet, leaving Admiral Yi resting at peace on the bench.

Yi Wan removed his own armor, handing it to Cristoph. He slid Admiral Yi's distinctive chest-piece over his head. Then he put on the helmet.

Carrie Anne thought that, from a distance, the nephew, Yi Wan, could certainly be mistaken for his famous uncle.

"Now what?" said Cristoph, who had put on Yi Wan's armor and was fussing with the unfamiliar straps.

"We do as my uncle commanded," said Yi Wan. "We beat the war drum. We chase the Japanese fleet out of Korea. And after they are gone, we will honor Admiral Yi and mourn his loss."

Chapter 10

"What happened next?" said Carrie Anne's father.

The grandfather clock in the hallway struck eight. Carrie Anne and her father sat at the old oak table in the kitchen. He was still drinking coffee but had switched to decaf.

Carrie Anne brushed a piece of hair out of her face with her good hand. Her other arm would have to be seen by a doctor but could wait till morning.

"Yi Wan chased down the Japanese fleet, rescuing the Chinese ally, General Chen," said Carrie Anne. She remembered the way General Chen had been so happy to see Admiral Yi coming to his aid and how his face had fallen when he found out that Admiral Yi was dead.

She continued the story. "After the battle ended, Yi Wan dropped us off on the shore of Namhae Island," said Carrie Anne.

"But how did Yi Wan survive the wreck of the turtle boat? And how did you get back to the present time?" said her father.

Carrie Anne could see the look of concern on her father's face. She'd been worried too. She'd never been stuck in the past before.

"Yi Wan was fished out of the water and held captive by the Japanese. He managed to escape while the they were attempting to board Admiral Yi's boat." Carrie Anne paused. "As far as how we got back to the present, I honestly don't know. As we walked inland, I crossed and uncrossed my fingers so many times. Nothing changed. But when we finally walked out of the woods, we were standing on a road, just like that." She snapped her fingers. "We called a taxi and got a ride back to Busan. We jumped on the train, and here we are."

"Hmm," said her father, thinking deeply about her story. "I hope Cristoph's grandparents weren't too worried. And his mother? I wouldn't like to get a call from her."

"That's just it," said Carrie Anne. "We came back to the present at nearly the same time as we'd left. Cristoph told his grandparents that one of us had gotten sick." Carrie Anne shrugged her hurt arm. The story was more or less true.

"I'm concerned about your time-sight, Carrie Anne," said her father. "It kept all three of you in the past against your will and in terrible danger."

Carrie Anne didn't respond right away. She thought about what her father said.

"That's true," she said, finally, "but I think the time-sight does what it does on purpose. In Gyeongju it helped us to save the lion statue. And in Namhae we were there at the right time to help Yi Wan finish the war for his uncle, Admiral Yi Sun-sin."

Her father shook his head in mild amazement. "The Admiral's statue sits outside the American embassy. I see it every day on the way in and out of work. Does it look anything like him?"

Carrie Anne thought about the stout statue that guarded the road leading to Gyeongbuk Palace, sitting as it did near the American Embassy. The statue depicted Admiral Yi in his armor, sitting at the ready.

"The statue is impressive," said Carry Anne, thoughtfully. "But the man himself was more impressive, kind and more humble than the statue shows."

"I see," said her father. "He sounds like a great man."

Carrie Anne couldn't disagree.

Her father continued, "You know, Carrie Anne, that you also have General Lee in our family tree. Your great-great-great uncle Robert E. Lee fought in the Civil War."

Carrie Anne hadn't known.

"From what I've read, our General Lee and your Admiral Yi had a lot in common."

Carrie Anne made a mental note to read more about her relative, General Lee. And she vowed to look up the history on Yi Wan, to see if the books could shed any light on the rest of his life. In an odd way she missed the brave young captain.

She remembered his hand on the tiller of the burning turtle boat and, at the end, as he beat the war drum wearing his uncle's armor.

Carrie Anne shook her head. Lauren was the one who wanted a serious relationship, not Carrie Anne. And it wasn't as though she could have one with a historic figure anyway. As her father often reminded her, she was only twelve-years old.

Maybe in a year or two she'd be ready for something serious. Fourteen was definitely more mature than twelve.

As for her time-sight, Carrie Anne remained more determined than ever to master the gift. The Coptic Christian priests had blessed her with time-sight for a reason—to help people.

Carrie Anne wanted to help people. All she really needed was practice, lots and lots of practice.

As her father sipped his coffee, Carrie Anne smiled, thinking about all the historic places in Seoul where she could practice and of what she might see there.

Postcards from Korea:

Historical Note

To My Dearest Nieces and Nephews,

When you come to see us in Korea, we may visit Namhae Island, one of the prettiest places in the country.

We spent a fun weekend in Namhae Island. We stayed in a *minbak*, which is a traditional Korean room that you can rent like a hotel. Normally a *minbak* includes a small kitchen, which makes it affordable for family vacations. We stayed in Daraengi Village, which is the one mentioned by Cristoph. It has row upon row of rice paddies that go in steps toward the ocean. Our *minbak* was an old farmhouse. Staying in a *minbak* really gives you a feel for what life was like in Korea many years ago.

There's lots to see on Namhae Island. My favorite thing on Namhae is the life-sized replica of a Turtle Boat.

Turtle Boats were invented (based on an earlier design) by Admiral Yi

Sun-sin. Instead of a wooden deck, they had a metal roof lined with sharp spikes to repel boarders. This was nearly 300 years before the famous battle between the Yankee and Confederate ironclads the Monitor and the Merrimac (1862).

The Turtle Boats could move much better and faster than the enemy ships. They were also designed to ram other ships. If you see a Turtle Boat, you'll notice a wooden dragon on the front. They would make smoke come out of the dragon's mouth. Can you imagine facing down a spiked metal ship with a flaming dragon's mouth trying to ram you? It would be scary!

Admiral Yi used the Turtle Boats to great effect against the Japanese invaders. But as with many military leaders, his success in battle created problems in his personal life. He became so popular that the rulers were afraid he might take over the country. Actually, Admiral Yi could have taken over, but he didn't, which is a testimony to his humility and greatness. Of course, when the Japanese invaded again, the rulers were all too quick to call upon Admiral Yi to defend the country.

The battle that took place at Noryang Strait was one of Admiral Yi's greatest victories.

I took a little bit of liberty with the history of the battle. The Japanese ships came through the strait that runs between Namhae Island and the Korean peninsula, but there is no indication that they fought Yi Wan's Turtle Boat at that time. Nor was that young man captured. He fought bravely alongside his uncle, Admiral Yi Sun-sin.

The naval battle raged along the west coast of Namhae Island. The Japanese had more ships than the Koreans. But Admiral Yi ambushed them. He attacked as they came through the Noryang Strait.

Because a strait is a narrow strip of water, only a few Japanese ships could join the attack. Admiral Yi's strategy eliminated the Japanese strength in numbers. Also, the Korean cannons were better than those of the Japanese. It was a wonderful plan. But as your great-grandfather, the World War II and Korean War veteran, could have told you, no plan survives the start of a battle. Things change very rapidly.

In the battle of Noryang Strait, things went badly for the Korean forces when their Chinese allies decided to attack directly. If Admiral Yi hadn't acted quickly, the Chinese general would have been cut off by the Japanese ships. Thus began a bloody hand-to-hand, ship-to-ship battle.

During the battle, Admiral Yi was shot. The wound was deadly. The Admiral knew he was dying. Yet his concern remained for his soldiers. He didn't want his forces to be demoralized by news of his death. So he said, tell no one of my death and keep beating the war drums.

Yi Wan put on his uncle's armor and continued to fight, maintaining the pretense that Admiral Yi yet lived.

After the battle, the Japanese fleet was nearly destroyed, much the same as happened to the French at Trafalgar.

There's a nice museum on Namhae Island that shows a movie about the battle. From the museum you can walk out to a point to see the place where Admiral Yi died. There are also several other historic sites nearby.

I hope you'll look up Admiral Yi on the internet and learn more about him. He's a lot like our own General Robert E. Lee, who many of your relatives are named after, including me. =)

Much love to you. Come visit us in Korea whenever you can.

Love,

Your Family in the Republic of Korea

Guest Art

Carrie Anne as drawn by Carla Reeve
www.carlamreeve.wix.com/folio

About David Lee

Hi! Thanks for reading this book. I hope it made your day a little better.

As you can see, I love history and hope to share a little bit of Korean history with you.

I live in the quiet town of Hunghae in the Republic of Korea with my wife and many children.

If you imagine Korea as a bunny rabbit, we live at the tip of its fluffy tail. (Korean people prefer to imagine Korea as a curled up tiger. They have big imaginations.)

I've been teaching at Handong Global University since 2007.

We love living in Korea. I grew up in the Smoky Mountains in Tennessee and my wife grew up in Virginia Beach; so we really like Hunghae, where the mountains slope down into some beautiful, rocky beaches.

By the way, I write other books under the pen-name Hans Hergot. Most of these are for adults, but some are for children. Please visit my site at

www.hanshergot.com.

You can buy my books, including this one, in print or electronically wherever books are sold.

Read more at:
www.CarrieAnneinKorea.com

Other Books

Carrie Anne in Korea (Book 3)
Princess Palace

Carrie Anne and Min meet the last Crown Princess of Korea and help her make a most difficult choice!

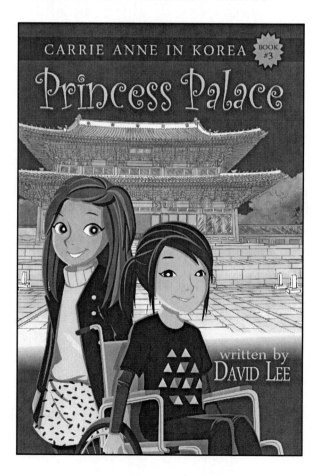

David Lee writing as Hans Hergot
Legends of Gyoll
Somewhere between Peter Rabbit and
Narnia lies the World of Gyoll, a cold
world of talking animals.
A read-aloud book for all ages.

CPSIA information can be obtained
at www.ICGtesting.com
Printed in the USA
LVOW12s1306210917
549557LV00001B/6/P